POKÉMON ™

Ash's Epic Island Challenge

By Simcha Whitehill

Ash's Epic Island Challenge

Written by Simcha Whitehill

The Prima Games logo and Primagames.com are registered trademarks of Penguin Random House LLC, registered in the United States. Prima Games is an imprint of DK, a division of Penguin Random House LLC, New York.

DK/Prima Games, a division of Penguin Random House LLC
6081 East 82nd Street, Suite #400
Indianapolis, IN 46250

ISBN: 978-0-7440-1946-9 (Paperback)
ISBN: 978-0-7440-1950-6 (Hardback)

Printing Code: The rightmost double-digit number is the year of the book's printing; the rightmost single-digit number is the number of the book's printing. For example, 18-1 shows that the first printing of the book occurred in 2018.
21 20 19 18   4 3 2 1

01-311218-Aug/2018
Printed and bound by Lake Book.

Credits

Publishing Manager
Tim Cox

Book Designer
Tim Amrhein

Production Designer
Wil Cruz

Production
Beth Guzman

Prima Games Staff

VP
Mike Degler

Publisher
Mark Hughes

Licensing
Paul Giacomotto

Marketing Manager
Jeff Barton

Digital Publisher
Julie Asbury

Table of Contents

Pokémon Reader: Ash's Epic Island Challenge

"Morning!" Rotom Dex rings as Ash's alarm.

However, Rotom Dex is surprised to find Ash is already awake. Ash is too excited for today to sleep in! Instead of catching some extra Zzzs, he has set a big goal for some other Zs. Ash is hoping to earn a special Z-Crystal for his Z-Ring so he can use a super powerful Z-Move.

"I can't wait until I can use a Z-Move again!" Ash says.

Over breakfast, Ash discusses his dream to earn a Z-Crystal with Rotom Dex and Professor Kikui, his teacher at the Pokémon School.

"You're as fired up as if you were hit by a Blast Burn!" Professor Kikui says to Ash.

There are many ways to get a Z-Crystal and none of them are easy. With the advice of Professor Kikui and Rotom Dex, Ash comes up with his strategy. It will be a direct, but difficult path to accomplish his goal.

Or as bold Ash puts it, "First some littler trials, then boom!"

Step number one to his plan, Ash will be put to the test in an Island Challenge. If he succeeds, the Kahuna of Melemele Island will accept this battle challenge for a Grand Trial. Then, if he wins their match, Ash will be awarded a new Z-Crystal.

"I think we should go pay a visit to Hala, the Kahuna of Melemele Island," Professor Kikui offers to kick things off.

"All right! Let's go!" Ash says ready to give it his all.

"Pika!" Pikachu cheers right behind its best buddy.

So, Professor Kikui, Ash, and Pikachu hit the road to find Hala. However, they aren't the only ones on the move.

A huge group of Alolan Rattata and Alolan Raticate are on a rampage, chowing down on a field full of fruit.

"Rrrr rara," the Alolan Rattata and Alolan Raticate growl as they enjoy their tasty treats.

When the farmer spots them in his fields, the feasting Pokémon scurry through the road to make their escape. But the Alolan Rattata and Alolan Raticate almost run into a big truck led by Tauros. The truck stops just in time, but out spills its large haul of logs. The wood is blocking the road so no one can pass, including Professor Kikui, Ash, and Pikachu.

Luckily, help arrives on the scene. Officer Jenny redirects traffic and a strong man comes to lift the logs out of the road.

"This gentleman is Hala," Professor Kikui tells Ash, "the Island Kahuna."

 Ash and Pikachu try to pitch in, but they cannot seem to pick up a single log together. Hulking Hala is carrying a few at a time. Still, that will not scare Ash from challenging the mighty Kahuna.

Soon, Hala along with his pal Hariyama and a helpful team of Machamp have all the logs loaded back on the truck.

Ash seizes the moment to approach Hala.

"Kahuna," Ash says proudly, "I'm here for the Island Challenge."

"I am well aware of that," the Kahuna says with a smile. The Kahuna explains that Ash is wearing a Z-Ring he made.

Late one night, a very important visitor—the Legendary Guardian Pokémon of Melemele Island, Tapu Koko, took the Z-Ring and Z-Crystal without telling Hala. Tapu Koko then gifted the pair to Ash.

"This is the first time Tapu Koko's ever taken a Z-Ring, that's for sure," Hala told Ash. "It appears Tapu Koko has a strong interest in you, young man."

While Ash was given his first Z-Crystal as a present, he will have to work hard to earn his second. To prove himself, Hala has just the puzzle for Ash to solve.

Hala tells Ash that a bunch of wild Alolan Rattata and Alolan Raticate have been causing trouble on Melemele Island.

"If you were the person being asked to solve this problem, what would you do?" Hala asks.

Ash replies confidently with a battle challenge. He offers to take on the whole group of Alolan Rattata and Alolan Raticate with his Pokémon pals Pikachu and Rowlet!

But Hala knows that there is a better answer and a better way.

Hala explains to Ash the purpose of the Island Challenge tradition. Its goal is to teach young people to love and protect the beautiful nature and Pokémon of Alola. He tells Ash to use his mind and his heart to come up with a solution.

"I want you to look for answers that won't only lead you to battle," Hala explains telling Ash to take some time to think it over.

Back in class, Ash has his head down on his desk. He is racking his brain, but he cannot seem to find a solution. Ash lets out a big sigh.

"I calculate that was his seven hundred and eighty-sixth sigh since speaking with Kahuna Hala yesterday," Rotom Dex points out.

Ash's classmates Lana, Lillie, Mallow, Kiawe, and Sophocles are surprised to see him so frustrated. They gather around Ash's desk and offer to help him.

Ash feels lucky to have these caring new friends in Alola. He knows if they put their heads together, they will come up with the perfect solution.

So, Ash tells his classmates all about his Island Challenge puzzle—the group of wild Alolan Rattata and Alolan Raticate.

To get more information on these Pokémon, Lillie wisely asks Rotom Dex what it knows about them.

Rotom Dex explains, "Long ago, Rattata and its evolved form, Raticate, came here to the Alolan Islands aboard cargo ships.

The numbers of Alolan Rattata and Alolan Raticate eventually grew so large that Yungoos and Gumshoos were brought in from a different region to chase them off."

"That's it!" Ash and his pals agree.

Now, a man with a plan, Ash races back to tell Hala his idea. He tells the Kahuna he wants to ask Yungoos and Gumshoos to help chase the Alolan Raticate and Alolan Rattata off again.

"Now that's a thoughtful and wise answer, Ash," Hala replies. "It is my answer, too."

"All right!" Ash exclaims, but he has one more important point to add. Ash tells Hala that he came to the idea with the help of his friends at school. He is nervous Hala will be upset with him, but Ash wants to be honest. To Ash's surprise, Hala is impressed.

"When we are searching for life's answers, we should always look to our friends for help," Hala assures Ash.

Hala then leads Ash through the lush Alolan forest. They arrive at the cave where he will begin his trial. Inside, live many Yungoos and Gumshoos.

One Gumshoos is so big and powerful it is known as the Totem Pokémon—a special Pokémon who assists Trainers during their Island Challenge. But first, Ash must earn the respect of the Totem Gumshoos.

Hala explains, "Ash, your trial is to take on the Totem Pokémon in a Pokémon battle and be victorious! Then, with the aid of the Totem Pokémon, I want you to chase away the Alolan Rattata and Alolan Raticate."

Hala calls out into the cave announcing Ash and the beginning of his first Island Challenge. Soon, a Gumshoos and Yungoos appear. They are the Totem Pokémon's allies. Ash will have to win a battle with them before the Totem Gumshoos will accept his challenge.

"I'm Ash Ketchum from Pallet Town! I'm asking you for a battle!" Ash bravely begins.

"Pika pika!" it adds at the ready.

Ash calls on his Electric-type pal Pikachu and his Grass- and Flying-type friend Rowlet to battle Normal-types Yungoos and Gumshoos. But when Rowlet arrives on the battlefield, it is asleep.

"Wake up!" Ash pleads.

Rowlet opens its eyes and sees the snarling Yungoos and Gumshoos

staring right at it. It yelps with surprise! Now, Rowlet is ready to snap into action.

Before Ash can make his first move, Gumshoos and Yungoos have wrapped Rowlet and Pikachu up in a swirling Sand Attack. Under the cover of dust, Yungoos and Gumshoos use Take Down to land a direct hit.

But Rowlet and Pikachu are not going to take this challenge lying down.

Yungoos and Gumshoos try to take another bite out of the battle with Hyper Fang. Pikachu and Rowlet quickly dodge it. Then, Ash calls on Rowlet to send a Leafage storm.

"You're not the only ones who can hide in your moves!" Ash warns.

While whirling Leafage covers the cave, Pikachu slaps Gumshoos with its tough Iron Tail. Whack!

Rowlet smartly snuck up behind Yungoos to strike it with Tackle. Thwap!

With that amazing combination, Yungoos and Gumshoos are unable to continue. But the real battle has just begun as the Totem Gumshoos appears with a hearty growl.

"Unreal! This one is three times the size of the previous Gumshoos!" Rotom Dex remarks.

Totem Gumshoos does not waste a moment launching into fiery red Frustration. Pikachu responds with a bright Thunderbolt, but Totem Gumshoos breaks right through it.

"Pikaaaaaaaa!" it yelps as it gets thrown by the wake of Gumshoos' fierce Frustration.

Ash has Rowlet follow up with another terrific Tackle, but the Totem Gumshoos is too fast to take the hit. Then, Totem Gumshoos picks up a rock to knock Rowlet out of the battle with Fling.

"Thanks a lot, Rowlet!" Ash says hugging his Pokémon pal. "Take a rest."

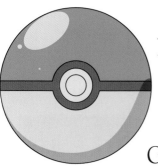

Rowlet returns to its Poké Ball. Pikachu remains ready to battle. It builds a bright Electro Ball, but Totem Gumshoos sends it flying straight at the cave wall with a windy Sand Attack. Then, Totem Gumshoos wallops Pikachu with a powerful Fire Punch.

"Piiiiika!" it cries, taking the hit.

When Totem Gumshoos stirs up yet another Sand Attack, Ash thinks fast. He has Pikachu use Quick Attack to hide itself in the sandstorm and surprise the giant Totem Gumshoos.

"All right, Pikachu, use Thunderbolt!" Ash adds.

"Piiiiikaaaachuuuuuu!"
it shouts, shooting a big
Thunderbolt blast.

Pow! Totem Gumshoos is left
unable to battle.

With that incredible zap, Hala declares
Ash's victory in the match. Ash and Pikachu
cheer, but the celebration is cut short.
Totem Gumshoos is struggling to get back
on its feet. Ash rushes over to help the
huge Pokémon.

"Are you all right, Gumshoos?" Ash worries.

Totem Gumshoos proudly stands up. It is so touched by Ash's concern and impressed by his battle skills that it gifts Ash a Z-Crystal.

"Wow!" Ash exclaims. "Thanks a lot!"

"For a Totem Pokémon to give a challenger a Z-Crystal is a very rare thing.

There is no doubt Ash must be a most unusual boy," Hala thinks to himself.

Ash has come for a purpose, even beyond earning a Z-Crystal. He has not forgotten his true Island Challenge task—to save Alola from the groups of Alolan Rattata and Alolan Raticate. Ash asks the Totem Gumshoos for its aid in chasing them away again. It nods its head, ready to uphold its duty.

They hear that the Alolan Rattata and Alolan Raticate are now raiding a local grocery store, eating everything in sight. Officer Jenny is on the scene and happy to see help has arrived in  the form of Ash Ketchum with the aid of the Totem Gumshoos.

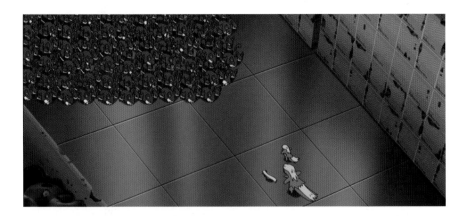

Inside the store, Totem Gumshoos, along with its allies Gumshoos and Yungoos, charge at the crowd of chomping Pokémon. The Alolan Raticate and Alolan Rattata are spooked to see them and immediately stop chewing.

Next, Totem Gumshoos sends its spiraling Sandstorm. The Alolan Rattata and Alolan Raticate are swept up and tossed out of the store. Afraid of another attack, the Alolan Rattata and Alolan Raticate continue to run right out of town!

"I can't thank you enough!" Officer Jenny says.

"It's all because of the Totem Gumshoos team," Ash adds.

Hala congratulates Ash on successfully completing his first Island Challenge and restoring the balance of nature in Alola!

"As Kahuna of the island of Melemele, I'm very happy to verify that you have indeed passed the trial," Hala said proudly.

As a reward, Ash will now have the chance to battle Hala in his first Grand Trial. Not only will he get to use his new Z-Crystal to make a Z-Move, if he wins the battle he will be awarded another Z-Crystal by the Kahuna.

"I'm really looking forward to it!" Ash tells Hala. "Right, buddy?"

"Pikachu!" it cheers ready to take on their next battle challenge together.

QUIZ

1. Who is the Kahuna of Melemele Island?

2. Which Pokémon are on a rampage in the story?

3. Which Pokémon took the Z-Ring and Z-Crystal from Hala?

4. Who does Ash fight in the first Pokémon challenge? (HINT: They are the Totem Pokémon's allies.)

5. Who fights alongside Pikachu?

Glossary

Ally
A person or group that is associated with another or others for a common cause.

Assist
To give support or aid to; help.

Calculate
To determine by mathematical methods; compute.

Evolve
Develop or change. In the Pokémon world, it's when a Pokémon changes into its next form.

Gift
To present (someone) with a gift.

Rampage
Violent and destructive behavior.

Seize
To take hold of suddenly.

Snarl
To growl viciously, like a dog.

Strategy
A plan for obtaining a specific goal.

Trial
An action performed in order to get results.

Answers to quiz:
1. Hala; 2. Alolan Rattata and Alolan Raticate; 3. Tapu Koko; 4. Gumshoos and Yungoos; 5. Rowlet.

31

A LEVEL FOR EVERY READER

This book is a part of an exciting four-level reading series to support children in developing the habit of reading widely for both pleasure and information. Each book is designed to develop a child's reading skills, fluency, grammar awareness, and comprehension in order to build confidence and enjoyment when reading.

Ready for a Level 3 (Beginning to Read Alone) book
A child should:
- be able to read many words without needing to stop and break them down into sound parts.
- read smoothly, in phrases and with expression, and at a good pace.
- self-correct when a word or sentence doesn't sound right or doesn't make sense.

A valuable and shared reading experience
For many children, reading requires much effort but adult participation can make reading both fun and easier. Here are a few tips on how to use this book with a young reader:

Check out the contents together:
- read about the book on the back cover and talk about the contents page to help heighten interest and expectation.
- ask the reader to make predictions about what they think will happen next.
- talk about the information he/she might want to find out.

Encourage fluent reading:
- encourage reading aloud in fluent, expressive phrases, making full use of punctuation and thinking about the meaning; if helpful, choose a sentence to read aloud to help demonstrate reading with expression.

Praise, share, and talk:
- notice if the reader is responding to the text by self-correcting and varying his/her voice.
- encourage the reader to recall specific details after each chapter.
- let her/him pick out interesting words and discuss what they mean.
- talk about what he/she found most interesting or important and show your own enthusiasm for the book.
- read the quiz at the end of the book and encourage the reader to answer the questions, if necessary, by turning back to the relevant pages to find the answers.

Series consultant, Dr. Linda Gambrell, Emerita Distinguished Professor of Education at Clemson University, has served as President of the National Reading Conference, the College Reading Association, and the International Reading Association.